SNOW WHITE

ROSE
RED

For Peter, who makes everything possible.
—Kelly Vivanco

Published in 2014 by Simply Read Books | www.simplyreadbooks.com
Illustrations © 2014 Kelly Vivanco

Library and Archives Canada Cataloguing in Publication

George, K. (Kallie), 1983-, author
Snow White and Rose Red / written by Wilhelm and Jacob
Grimm ; retold by Kallie George ; illustrated by Kelly Vivanco.

ISBN 978-1-927018-34-7 (bound)

I. Vivanco, Kelly, illustrator II. Grimm, Wilhelm, 1786-1859.
Schneewei¦Âchen und Rosenrot. III. Grimm, Jacob, 1785-1863.
Schneewei¦Âchen und Rosenrot. IV. Title.

PS8563.E6257S66 2014   jC813'.6   C2013-902918-4

We gratefully acknowledge for their financial support of our publishing program the Canada Council for the Arts, the BC Arts Council, and the Government of Canada through the Canada Book Fund (CBF).

Manufactured in Malaysia.

Book design by Heather Lohnes.

10 9 8 7 6 5 4 3 2 1

THE GRIMM BROTHERS'

SNOW WHITE & ROSE RED

ILLUSTRATED BY KELLY VIVANCO

as retold by Kallie George

SIMPLY READ BOOKS

there once was a poor widow who lived in a little cottage by the woods. In her front garden grew two beautiful intertwining rose bushes, one with white flowers, the other with red. The widow's two daughters were just like the rose bushes—different, but equally lovely.

Snow White's hair was white like the stars, while Rose Red's hair was as dark as the space between them. Snow White was quiet and gentle, while Rose Red was loud and lively. Snow White preferred to sit indoors and read while Rose Red liked to romp in the meadows and sing. But both girls were helpful, grateful and loving and never thought badly of anyone or anything.

When they went into the woods to pick berries, they fed rabbits clover from their hands. Deer grazed beside them, and birds perched on their shoulders and sang songs. If they stayed too long and it got dark, they would lie down beside each other and sleep on the moss until morning. Trusting and loving her girls, the widow never worried about them.

One morning, when they awoke after sleeping overnight in the woods, they saw before them a beautiful child in a white dress. The child stood silently and looked at them in a friendly way, then quickly disappeared into the forest. Looking around, they discovered they had been sleeping right next to a cliff and surely would have plunged over it if they had walked any farther in the dark. When they told their mother about it, she said the child must have been the angel who protects good children.

One stormy winter night, they were startled by a loud thumping at the door.

"Rose Red, please open it," said their mother. "It must be a traveler seeking shelter."

Rose Red hurried to the door, expecting to see some poor soul. But when a black bear stuck his head inside, she screamed and backed away. Snow White ran and hid under her mother's bed and Rose Red followed.

The bear spoke: "Please don't run. I won't hurt you. I am half-frozen to death and all I want to do is warm up."

"You poor creature," said the widow. "Come here and lie down beside our fire. But not too close, or your fur will be singed." Then she called to her daughters, "Come out, dears. This bear is not going to hurt us."

the girls crept out and stared at the giant beast. As the bear began to warm up, he asked them, "Would you please brush the lumps of snow from my fur?"

With shaking hands, the girls took out a whiskbroom and removed the snow. Little by little, they lost their fear of their strange guest. Cozy and content, the bear began to snore and the girls began to play with him. Rose Red walked with her bare feet on his back and tried to roll him over, while Snow White rubbed behind his ears and felt his soft fur between her fingers. The bear woke up and was good-natured about their play.

Later, the widow said to the bear, "You're welcome to stay the night if you wish."

And so he did. He left early the next morning, ambling through the snow into the woods. But the next night, he returned, as he did every night thereafter. The bear enjoyed romping with Rose Red, but most of all liked to fall asleep as Snow White gently combed his fur.

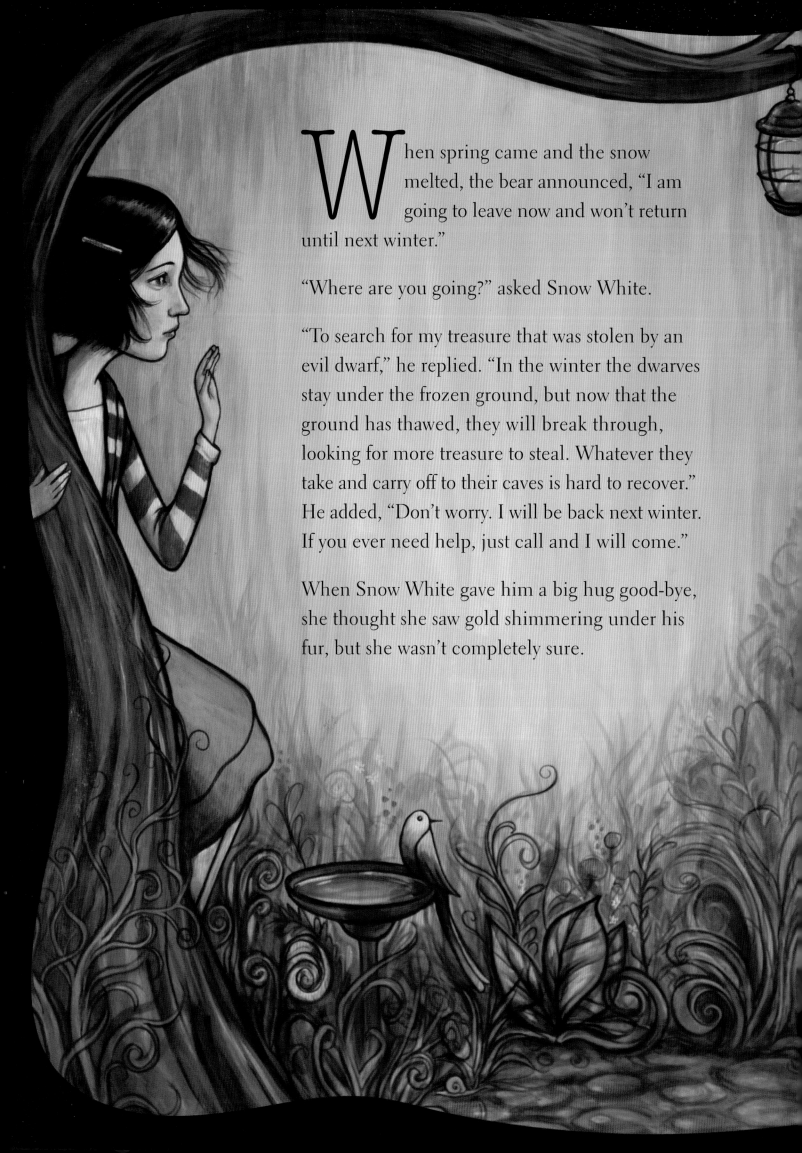

When spring came and the snow melted, the bear announced, "I am going to leave now and won't return until next winter."

"Where are you going?" asked Snow White.

"To search for my treasure that was stolen by an evil dwarf," he replied. "In the winter the dwarves stay under the frozen ground, but now that the ground has thawed, they will break through, looking for more treasure to steal. Whatever they take and carry off to their caves is hard to recover." He added, "Don't worry. I will be back next winter. If you ever need help, just call and I will come."

When Snow White gave him a big hug good-bye, she thought she saw gold shimmering under his fur, but she wasn't completely sure.

The next day, the widow sent her daughters out to fetch wood for the fire. Soon they came upon a big tree that had just been cut down. Beside it a strange small creature was jumping up and down in the grass. They couldn't figure out what it was until they came nearer and saw it was an old dwarf with a wrinkly face and a very long white beard. The tip of his beard was stuck in a crack of the tree trunk. He stared at Snow White and Rose Red with angry red eyes and screamed, "Why are you just standing there, you dumb dolts? Come here at once and help me!"

"What happened?" asked Rose Red.

"Can't you see?" he shouted. "I was splitting this big tree trunk to get some firewood. I drove my wedge in but it popped right out of the wood and the crack closed and caught me. Now my beautiful beard is stuck and you two just stand there and laugh."

O f course, the girls were not laughing at all. They pulled as hard as they could on his beard, but it was stuck fast.

"Don't you have any better ideas?" cried the dwarf.

"Yes," said Snow White. She took a small pair of scissors from her pocket and handed them to Rose Red, who snipped a bit of the dwarf's beard off.

As soon as he was free, the dwarf yelled, "You beastly brats, how could you cut off the tip of my beautiful beard?" Then he grabbed a small sack hidden between the roots of the tree and ran off without a thank you or a good-bye.

"How strange," said Rose Red. But thinking no more of it, they continued with their task.

few days later, Snow White and Rose Red went to the brook to catch some fish for supper. As they approached, they saw what looked like a huge frog jumping up and down towards the water as if it was about to plunge in. They ran to see what was going on and immediately recognized the dwarf.

"What are you doing?" asked Rose Red. "Are you going swimming in the brook?"

"How could you think that, you gullible goose?" screamed the dwarf. "Can't you see that a fish is about to pull me in? I was just sitting here fishing when the wind tangled my beard in my line. Come here at once and help me."

Rose Red grabbed his arms to keep him on the shore, while Snow White tried to untangle his beard from the line. It was hopeless. There was only one thing they could do. Again, Snow White took out her scissors and handed them to Rose Red, who snipped off a bit of the beard.

As soon as he was free, the dwarf yelled, "You terrible twits, how could you disfigure me like this? Wasn't it cruel enough to clip the end of my beard? Now you've cut off the best part." Then he grabbed a medium-sized sack hidden in the rushes beside the brook and ran off, again without a thank you or a good-bye.

"Even stranger," said Snow White. But again, thinking no more of it, they continued with their task.

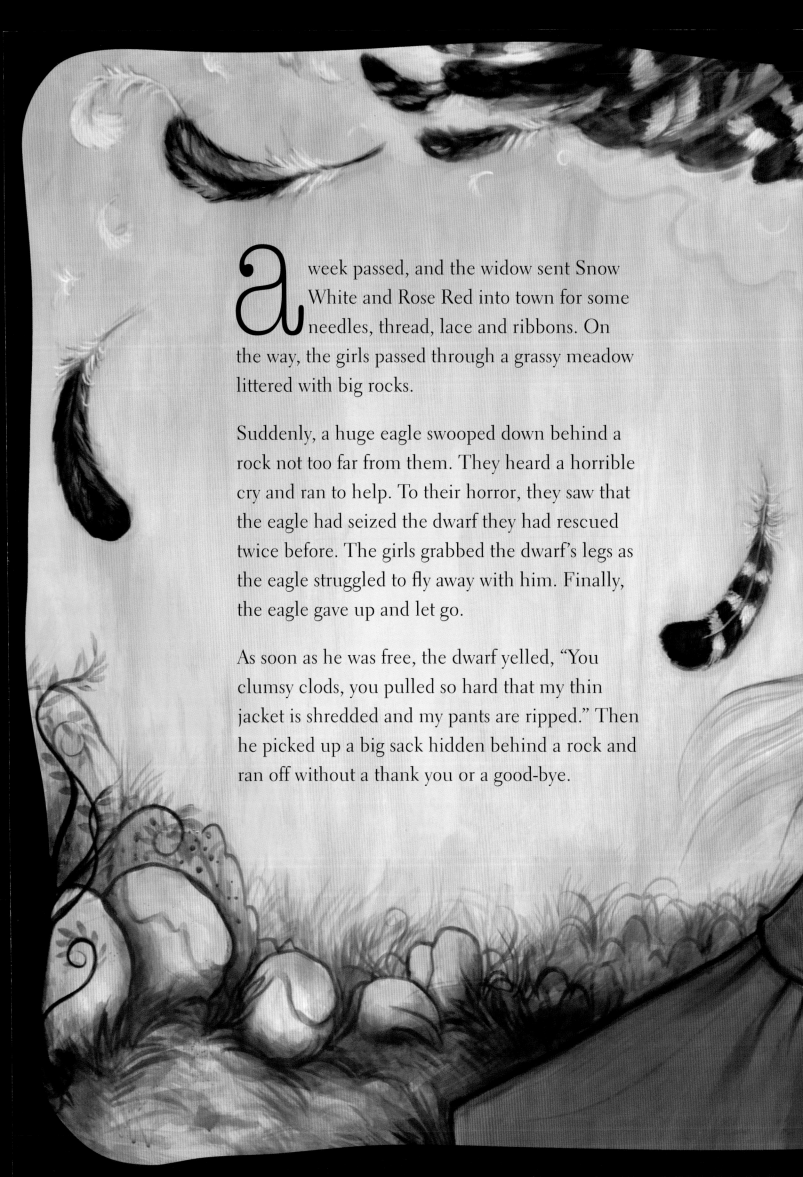

a week passed, and the widow sent Snow White and Rose Red into town for some needles, thread, lace and ribbons. On the way, the girls passed through a grassy meadow littered with big rocks.

Suddenly, a huge eagle swooped down behind a rock not too far from them. They heard a horrible cry and ran to help. To their horror, they saw that the eagle had seized the dwarf they had rescued twice before. The girls grabbed the dwarf's legs as the eagle struggled to fly away with him. Finally, the eagle gave up and let go.

As soon as he was free, the dwarf yelled, "You clumsy clods, you pulled so hard that my thin jacket is shredded and my pants are ripped." Then he picked up a big sack hidden behind a rock and ran off without a thank you or a good-bye.

by now Snow White and Rose Red were used to his ingratitude. They shrugged their shoulders and merrily continued on their way to the village to do their shopping.

Later, on their way home, while they were passing through the same meadow, they were surprised to see the dwarf again. He was even more surprised to see them, for he had just emptied his big sack of jewels and was inspecting them.

The setting sun shone on the sparkling stones, making them glitter and glow. The girls stopped in their tracks, mesmerized by their beauty.

"Why are you staring at my treasure?" the dwarf screamed, his face turning scarlet with rage. "You're planning to steal it, you wicked wretches. I'll get you!"

He picked up a pointed stick and lunged towards them.

"Help! Help!" they cried, jumping back.

Their voices echoed through the woods where their friend the bear was roaming. He heard them and remembered his promise.

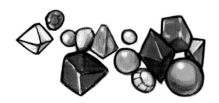

all of a sudden, there was a loud growling and a huge black bear dashed out of the woods towards the dwarf.

The dwarf cried out in terror. "Not you!" He stumbled backwards. "Here, take the treasure! Take all of it back! But don't eat me. Eat those girls instead. They are as fat as young quail and will make a tasty feast. Go after them quickly or they'll get away!"

Ignoring the dwarf's ranting, the bear charged him. With one powerful blow of his paw, he knocked the dwarf down dead.

Snow White and Rose Red didn't see this, for they were fleeing across the meadow as fast as they could go. The bear called out, "Snow White! Rose Red! Don't be afraid. Stop! Wait for me and I will walk home with you."

the girls recognized the voice at once. They stopped and turned around to greet their friend. As he approached them, his furry hide fell away and before them stood a handsome young man dressed in a golden cloak.

Snow White and Rose Red were speechless.

"I am the son of a king," he explained to them, "and that wicked dwarf stole my treasure last year. He turned me into a wild bear, and his death was the only way to break the spell. Don't feel sorry for him, for he earned his fate. Thank you for helping me."

"Thank you. You saved us from him," said Rose Red. "But I hope, in the world beyond, he will find happiness."

"And peace," chimed in Snow White. For the girls couldn't think badly or wish harm upon anyone, even the ungrateful dwarf.

"Perhaps he will," said the prince. "But your happiness, I promise, shall only grow in measure."

and so it was true. Snow White married the prince. Rose Red, who at first did not wish to marry, eventually fell in love with the prince's younger brother, who was gentle and sweet like her sister.

the girls invited their mother to live with them in the joy and comfort of the castle. When she moved, the widow took cuttings from the two rose bushes that grew in front of their old cottage and planted them in front of her bedroom window. Every year thereafter the bushes bore the most vivid red and white roses, different but equally lovely in every bloom.

THE END